This Book Belongs To

_____

It all started with the first climb ...

May The Magnificent Lighthouse
is a story written about Cape May Lighthouse in beautiful Cape
May, New Jersey. This story is the first of five delightful
children's books in the Southern New Jersey Lighthouse Series.
Each book is filled with a variety of important and meaningful
lessons. The series not only touches on the history of the
individual lighthouses, but also teaches the importance of working
together to protect our rich maritime history. The pages are filled
with the spirit of cooperation, showing the amazing things that
can be accomplished if people are willing to work together.
There is also the visual and artistic aspect. Each dazzling page is
illustrated with full and colorful fine art watercolor paintings.
Thus helping each reader better appreciate fine art.
In addition to teaching history, cooperation, and fine art
appreciation, each story features a different letter. This fun
addition to each book makes them an interesting way to teach
reading and vocabulary skills.

May, the Magnificent Lighthouse features the letter "M".
As young Ella climbs Cape May Lighthouse
with the help of her new friend, Mac the Mouse,
her questions lead her on a marvelous journey
of discovery and adventure. She finds herself learning lessons
she will never forget.

And so it begins ...

May The Magnificent Lighthouse

By Nancy Patterson

Dedicated to my faithfully supportive family
especially my granddaughter Ella
who inspired the writer within me

Very special thanks to friends & family for all their support!

Published by Bayberry Cottage Gallery
* Mauricetown, New Jersey *
to contact or view more work by Nancy Patterson please visit ...
http://nancy-patterson.artistwebsites.com

May, the magnificent lighthouse,
Majestically stands straight and tall.
Surrounded by marsh and the ocean,
May faithfully keeps watch over all.

The light at May's top shines bright in the sky,
While migrating shore birds go flying by.
May guides each ship, marks the mouth of the bay,
Makes a clear way, both by night and by day.
Each month after month and each year after year,
Many ships have sailed by without any fear.

As I looked up at May, questions came to mind.
I wondered if May was just one of a kind.
What kept May's light burning for so very long?
What made Cape May Light so majestic and strong?
Maybe May herself held the answers I seek;
But how could I ask her when I am so meek?

While mulling along coming up with a plan,
I spotted a mouse hiding in the moist sand.
"Do you think I'd be a bother," I said to the mouse.
"If I asked questions of May, the massive lighthouse?
My questions are honest; they aren't at all bad.
Asking May some questions shouldn't make her mad.

May looks rather wise and doesn't look at all mean,
Though her great size is taller than ever I've seen.
I could mail all my questions or shout really loud,
Maybe then May would hear me up there in the clouds."
As I mumbled my questions not expecting reply,
The miniature mouse looked me right in the eye.

Then to my great surprise what came out of his mouth,
Was a way to find out about May, the lighthouse.
With a mild voice he said, "My name is Mac
And I may have the many answers you lack.
To find them you don't have to be very tall.
You don't have to be massive or mighty at all.

Inside of May's tower is a marvelous staircase.
You can climb all the way up at your very own pace.
There are pictures inside that tell of May's history.
See for yourself; they might solve your great mystery."
I held back my surprise and said, "I'd love to climb May.
I can't think of a better way to spend this fine day."

"March on", said Mac as he scurried and leapt,
Making his way to the very first step.
As I stood at the bottom with much on my mind,
Mac explained that each lighthouse was one of a kind.
He said, "Their flashes are different for ships to see,
Shining bright over miles for both you and for me."

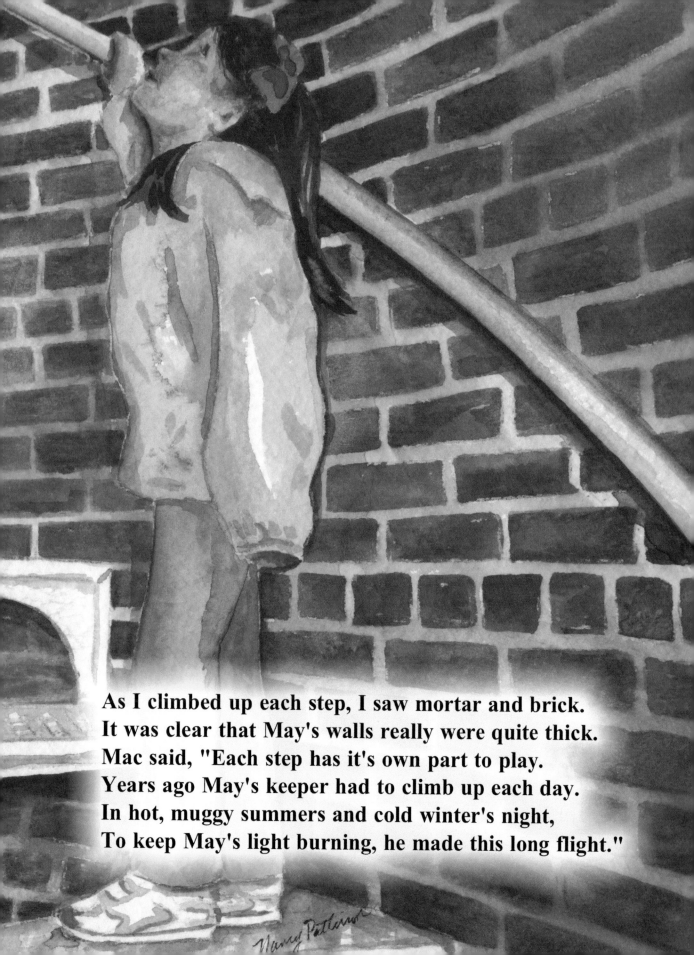

As I climbed up each step, I saw mortar and brick.
It was clear that May's walls really were quite thick.
Mac said, "Each step has it's own part to play.
Years ago May's keeper had to climb up each day.
In hot, muggy summers and cold winter's night,
To keep May's light burning, he made this long flight."

May's work goes on; but it's not quite the same.
She now has another claim to her fame.
May not only marks a place by the shore;
May teaches us history and so much more -
Memories of strong storms, rough seas and strife,
A museum and monument to maritime life.

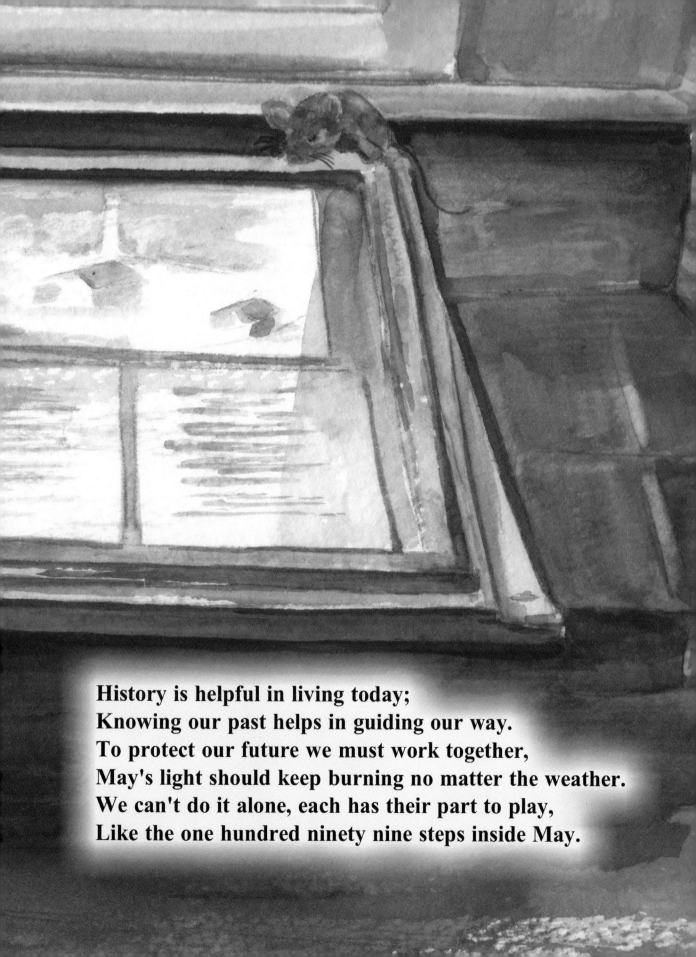

History is helpful in living today;
Knowing our past helps in guiding our way.
To protect our future we must work together,
May's light should keep burning no matter the weather.
We can't do it alone, each has their part to play,
Like the one hundred ninety nine steps inside May.

I soon got to the top like millions before.
My eyes filled with wonder as I went out the door.
The view from May's top was marvelous to see.
The lessons I learned were now a part of me.
So much I had learned from Mac, the small mouse.
Answers made clear as I climbed the lighthouse.

Many give their time to keep this lighthouse turning.
Each person who visits helps keep May's light burning.
I'm thankful so many protect our great past.
Together, we can all make sure it will last.
May's truly as magnificent as she can be,
Shining light on our history for all to see.

The History of Cape May Lighthouse

Cape May Lighthouse is the third lighthouse to mark the shore of the southern most tip of New Jersey. The first was built in 1823 and the second in 1847. The exact location of both the first and the second is now underwater due to erosion. The current lighthouse was completed in 1859 and was first lighted on October 31 of that same year. The tower is constructed with an inner and outer wall, making it strong enough to withstand hurricane strength winds. There are 199 steps in the tower and 217 in all. The lighthouse was dark during WW2 and the Fresnel lens was dismantled and replaced with a rotating Aero beacon in 1946. Today the Cape May Light remains an active lighthouse and is used as both a navigational aid as well as a museum. The beacon flashes every 15 seconds and is visible 24 miles out to sea. The tower is open to the public and may be climbed during favorable weather conditions. The Oil House is also open to the public and is used as a Museum Gift Shop.

CPSIA information can be obtained
at www.ICGtesting.com
Printed in the USA
LVIC060414110513
333329LV00002B